To Stafford Library —
Celebrating Isaac Cohen's 6th Birthday

Nov. 6, 1994

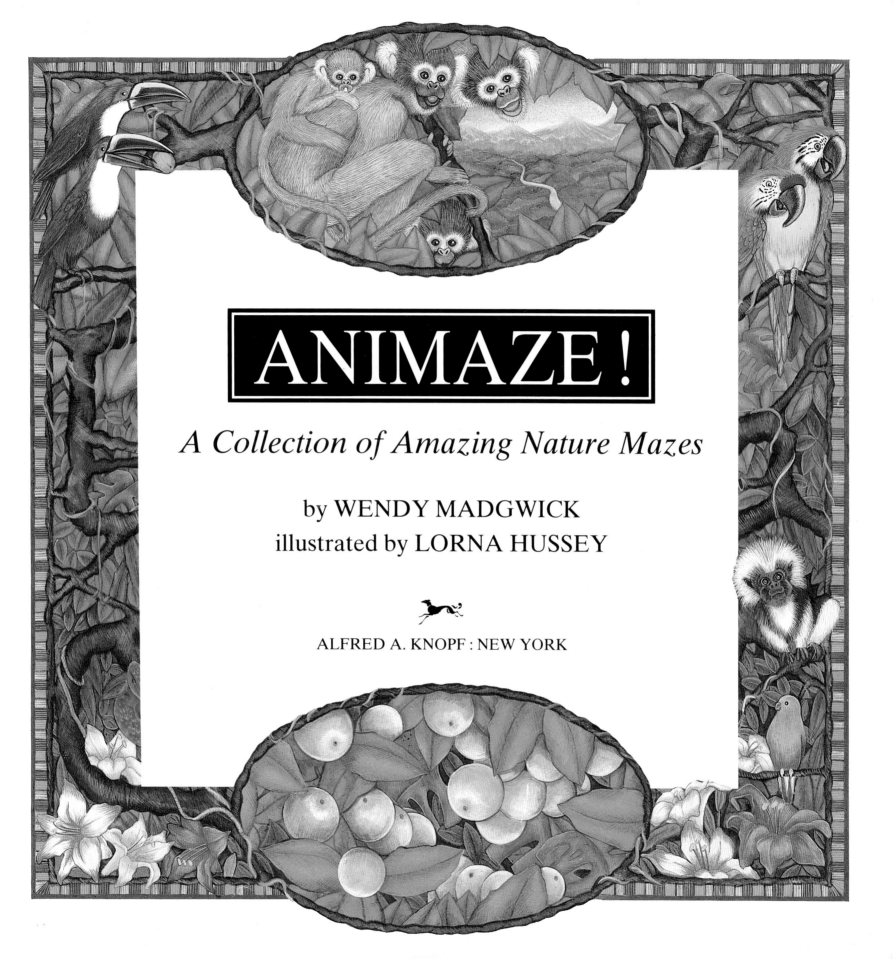

ANIMAZE !

A Collection of Amazing Nature Mazes

by WENDY MADGWICK

illustrated by LORNA HUSSEY

ALFRED A. KNOPF : NEW YORK

For my grandparents
Dan and Agnes Johnson — L.H.
For my family — W.M.

First American edition 1992.
Copyright © 1992 by The Templar Company plc.
All rights reserved under International and Pan-American Copyright Conventions.
Published in the United States by Alfred A. Knopf, Inc., New York.
Distributed by Random House, Inc., New York.

Devised and produced by The Templar Company plc.,
Pippbrook Mill, London Road, Dorking, Surrey RH4 1JE, Great Britain.

Designed by Janie Louise Hunt
Color separations by Positive Colour Ltd.,
Maldon, Essex, Great Britain.

Library of Congress Cataloging in Publication Data
Madgwick, Wendy
Animaze!: a collection of amazing nature mazes / by Wendy Madgwick;
illustrated by Lorna Hussey. — 1st American ed. p. cm.
Summary: Text and illustrations featuring mazes depict the
habitats and living conditions of animals worldwide.
1. Animals—Habitat—Juvenile literature. 2. Maze puzzles—Juvenile literature.
[1. Animals—Habitat.   2. Maze puzzles.   3. Puzzles.]
I. Hussey, Lorna, ill.   II. Title.
QL756.M23   1992   591.56'4—dc20   91-46892
ISBN 0-679-82665-3
ISBN 0-679-92665-8 (lib. bdg.)

Manufactured in Italy   10 9 8 7 6 5 4 3 2

Please help the animals!

A little zebra is lost in the grasslands. He's trying to reach his mother, but cheetahs are lurking nearby, and a hungry lioness is on the prowl.

You can help by finding the right path through the grassland maze and the other nature mazes in this book. Each maze is set in a different habitat — from the icy Arctic to the tropical jungles of South America. Trace the correct path with your finger. Along the way you'll meet lots of other animals — strange little fish that climb trees and walk on mud, a desert cat that can knock birds out of midair, and more. But be careful — the wrong path could mean trouble.

Solutions are at the back of the book, where you'll also find "nature notes" that will tell you all about the animals.

Better hurry — the little zebra misses his mom!

SWAMPLANDS

Silently the evening tide has swept into the mangrove swamps that surround Borneo, an island in Southeast Asia. Startled, a male proboscis monkey looks up as he hears the call of the other monkeys on the mainland. He has been exploring and is now stranded on a small island. The other monkeys are feeding along the shore and he wants to join in the feast. A strong swimmer, the monkey can weave his way through the water and get back to shore — but these paths are blocked by the tangled roots of the mangrove trees and the creatures that inhabit this strange world. Can you find the way back?

A WORLD IN MINIATURE

In the gloom of a South American jungle, tiny leaf-cutter ants
are slicing off pieces of leaf to take back to their underground nest.
Then they scuttle along the forest floor, following well-worn scent
trails that will lead them home. But they must be careful.
Many of their trails are blocked by other animals. A sticky-tongued
anteater is on the prowl, looking for a meal. Fierce-jawed soldier
termites block another path, and a tiny antbird is pecking its way
along another. Only one route leads home, but which one?
See if you can find the safe path back to the ants' nest.

UPSTREAM

At long last the exhausted salmon have reached their destination. They have traveled hundreds of miles across the sea to return to the North American river in which they were born. Now they must make their way upstream to the spawning grounds, where the females will lay their eggs. The journey is beset by many hazards — rockfalls block the way, and bears and ospreys fish for their dinner as otters and beavers swim and play in the streams. Follow the maze of waterways and see if you can find the route to the salmon's spawning ground. Only one stream is safe, however. All the rest lead to disaster.

DESERT WASTES

As the afternoon draws to a close and the shadows lengthen,
the animals of the Sahara desert make their way toward the oasis
for a much-needed drink of water and a meal of seeds and
insects. Some animals are already there, lapping up the cool
water. Other animals are on their way. Which animals reach the
oasis safely? Follow the hoofprints of the camel and oryx,
the pawprints of the fox and caracal, and the tiny marks left by
the jerboa and gerbil as they hop across the plain.
Which ones make it safely to the water hole?

ON THE RIVER

The river is bathed in the warm, hazy sunshine of an early summer's day. Suddenly the peace is broken by a sharp sound. The male beaver lifts his head to listen. There it is again: "Slap! Slap! Slap!" His mate is slapping her large, flattened tail on the water to warn of danger. Then, he knows, she will dive beneath the water with their two babies and seek the safety of their lodge deep within the dam. The male beaver must swim home quickly. But there are many animals on the river, and he does not want to disturb them. Can you find the way back to the dam? Follow the maze of waterways, but be careful — only one route is clear of all other creatures.

THE OUTBACK

The bark of a dingo as it calls to its pups echoes across the plains of the Australian outback. Startled, three little red kangaroos, called joeys, look up. They have become separated from their mothers. Frightened, they rush back to the safety of their mothers' pouches. But their way is blocked! Mallee fowls are nesting, and two young emus scratch at the grassy scrubland near their father. Termite mounds tower over the landscape, and the fearless thorny devil and Gould's goanna scuttle into the shade to escape the heat of the sun. Which joey belongs to which mother? Follow the trails and see if you can find out.

IN THE JUNGLE

High in the treetops of a South American jungle, a group
of chattering squirrel monkeys are traveling with their young in
search of food. Far below they see the juicy, golden fruit of
the guava tree. But their way is blocked by many animals that
are feeding and dozing in the heat of the day. They must
creep past the prowling jaguar and the menacing snakes that
sometimes eat small monkeys. They must not awaken the
sleeping ocelot. And they must not disturb the toucans and
macaws, whose noisy calls will alert every creature in the forest.
Follow the maze of large branches that lead to the fruit, but
be careful — it won't be easy, and only one route is safe.

AT THE WATER HOLE

Just after sunrise, before the baking sun rises high above the African savanna, or grasslands, many animals make their way to the water hole to drink. A young zebra has become separated from the herd as they traveled across the plains to quench their thirst. Wide-eyed, the foal looks out over the dusty grasslands. It can see the herd in the distance, but there are many dangers as well. Lions, cheetahs, and other hungry predators hide, waiting to pounce on unsuspecting prey. Hippos wallow, long-necked giraffes nibble at leafy trees, and wildebeest and deer graze. See if you can find the way to the water hole, but beware — only one path is safe.

ON THE REEF

Teeming with life, Australia's Great Barrier Reef is like an underwater jungle. Thousands of beautiful sea creatures live among the ornate and colorful corals. Here, the banded angelfish has been out foraging for food, but as evening falls, it seeks its shelter deep within the coral reef, near other angelfish. The fish heads for home, but its route is blocked by its enemies and by other creatures probing the crevices in search of food. Only one path is clear and will lead the angelfish safely home. Try to find it, but be careful — the eagle ray, shark, and octopus are waiting to pounce!

LIFE UNDERGROUND

Beneath the ground, in a warm, snug nest, six baby rabbits lie sleeping. A short time before, their mother had left them to gather food in the woods.

Now, as the sun begins to set and the moon rises high in the sky, she makes her way back to the burrow.

But it is not a simple journey. Many dangers await her. Prowling creatures in search of food block the entrances. Tunnels have collapsed or are occupied by other animals — some hunting her and her babies. Can you find the way back to the nest? Follow the tunnels through the maze of the rabbit warren, but beware — only one path is safe and leads to home.

PATHWAYS IN THE SNOW

Summer has come to the snowy wastes of the Arctic tundra.
Flowers bloom, insects buzz, and lemming mothers and their
pups enjoy the warm sunshine while they search for food along
the water's edge. As daylight fades, the lemming mothers realize
with alarm that they are far from home. They must get their pups
back to the burrow, but the way is blocked by grazing animals,
deep snowdrifts, and hungry enemies hunting for their supper.
The pups are too young to swim through the ice-cold water or
cross the freezing marsh. Instead, the mothers must travel over
the land. Can you help them? Find the way back to the lemmings'
burrow, but remember — only one path leads safely home.

TO THE SEA

In the hours before sunrise, on a lonely beach in Costa Rica, hundreds of newly hatched green turtles scrabble from their underground nests to the surface of the sand. They begin to make their way to the sea. But their journey is not easy. Some are confused by the twinkling lights of a nearby village, mistaking them for the moon glinting on the sea. Others fall prey to raccoons and coatis. Gulls hover overhead, waiting to swoop, and other shore creatures block the way. Some turtles even fall into the deep ruts made by a beach buggy as it churns its way across the wet sand. Can you tell which turtles will make it safely to the sea? Follow their trails and find out.

SWAMPLANDS

The mangrove swamps have once again been submerged by the incoming evening tide. A proboscis monkey must swim back to the jungle, but his path is blocked. The tangled roots of the mangrove trees sprout finger-like above the water, while the fearsome crocodile waits, jaws open, ready to pounce!

1. Proboscis monkeys They spend most of their time in the treetops feeding on leaves, fruit, and flowers. The male has a long, bulbous nose, which straightens out when he makes his loud, honking call.

2. Mudskipper These strange little fish can climb, walk, and skip over the mud. Their large mobile eyes help them to see well out of water, and they move by using their strong pectoral (shoulder) fins.

3. Fiddler crab The male fiddler crab has one small and one huge claw. Its small claw is used for feeding; its large claw plays a dual role. The claw is used as a weapon to warn off other males, and is waved invitingly to attract a passing female.

4. Crab-eating mongoose This mongoose hunts alone, usually at night, feeding on crabs and similar creatures. The mongoose marks the boundary of its den with a scent to warn away other animals.

5. Eurasian otter Now rare, these otters live in burrows in the riverbank. Good swimmers, they use their large, webbed hind feet and thick, muscular tails to propel them through the water. Their nostrils and ears can be closed when they are swimming.

6. Saltwater crocodile One of the largest and most dangerous of animals, the estuarine crocodile is hunted for its skin and is now protected in many areas. Able to live even in salt water, it rarely comes on land.

7. Great egret Like all herons, the egret hunts in water. It waits motionless until it sights its prey, which it then seizes in its strong, sharp beak.

8. Sea eagle Sometimes called fishing eagles, these large birds have rough surfaces on the underside of their toes to help them grasp their slippery prey.

9. Crab-eating macaques Mostly active during the day, these small, long-tailed monkeys live on the ground near water. They feed on crabs and other small animals.

10. Bearded pig These large pigs have white whiskers on their cheeks and large warts beneath their eyes. They feed on plants and fruit, often following groups of monkeys and picking up the food they drop.

11. Lesser mouse deer The smallest of the mouse deer, weighing only 4 pounds, these shy creatures mainly come out at night. They do not have horns or antlers, but the males have long upper canine teeth that hang down below their jaws.

12. Glossy ibis The most widespread ibis, it feeds on insects and water creatures. The female nests in a tree or reed bed, and both parents care for the eggs and young.

13. Osprey At breeding time, the osprey, or fish hawk, builds a large nest on the ground from sticks and seaweed. The same nest is often used year after year until it becomes huge. The male feeds the female while she incubates the eggs, and he helps feed the fledglings as well.

14. Mangrove snake Many of these rear-fanged snakes live at the swamp's edge, feeding on crabs and fish.

A WORLD IN MINIATURE

In the dense South American jungle, tiny leaf-cutter ants march back to their nests. But their way is blocked by many hazards, from hungry birds to the sticky-tongued anteater. Only one path leads safely to the nest.

1. Leaf-cutter ants These tiny jungle insects cut off pieces of leaf with their sharp jaws and take them back to their nest. They carry the pieces, often larger than themselves, over their heads like enormous umbrellas. Because of this, they are also called parasol ants.

2. Spiny pocket mouse These tiny, bristly mice, sometimes called rice rats, usually come out at night to feed on seeds.

3. Ocher-bellied flycatcher This active little bird flits from tree to tree seizing insects and spiders in its hook-tipped bill.

4. Giant armadillo The largest armadillo, weighing up to 130 pounds, it has an armored body with movable horny plates.

It feeds on ants and termites, smashing their hills with its large-clawed front feet and licking them up with its tongue.

5. Tropical centipedes These fast-moving creatures have a pair of poison claws (modified front legs) just behind their head. This tropical species can grow up to 12 inches long.

6. Praying mantis Motionless, mantises sit hidden among the greenery, with their legs held as if in prayer, waiting to pounce on their unsuspecting prey.

7. Long-horned beetles Their long antennae can be four times the length of their bodies. The grubs burrow into wood, weakening and spoiling it for building use.

8. Arrow poison frogs The brilliant colors of these tiny ground-dwelling frogs warn their enemies that they are poisonous. Local tribespeople extract the poison and use it on the tips of their arrows and blowpipe darts.

9. Antbirds These tiny birds, most of them less than 4 inches long, have strong, hooked beaks. Many live on the dense forest floor in Central and South America, feeding on ants and other insects.

10. Soldier termites Termites differ from ants in that when the young hatch, they look like small adults, not grubs. The powerful jaws of some soldier termites can snap an ant in half.

11. Horned frog As broad as it is long, this large-mouthed frog spends much of its life half-buried in the ground.

12. Iguana These agile tree-living lizards feed on plants, but they can defend themselves with sharp teeth and claws if attacked by predators.

13. Caecilian These strange limbless creatures look like giant earthworms but are in fact amphibians. They burrow into the soft soil of the forest floor in search of their prey of insects and earthworms and rarely appear above ground.

14. Giant anteater A giant anteater, walking on the knuckles of its front feet to protect its sharp claws, snuffles over the forest floor in search of food. Like the armadillo, it demolishes ant nests and termite mounds, then mops up the insects with its sticky tongue, which can extend up to 2 feet.

15. Anaconda One of the largest snakes at up to 37 feet long, the anaconda can climb small trees and shrubs but never strays far from water.

UPSTREAM

The salmon have swum hundreds of miles from the Atlantic Ocean to a river in North America. Their journey is almost at its end, but they still face many hazards, from osprey to bears. Only one waterway will lead them safely to the spawning grounds, where the female will lay her eggs.

1. Great egret During the breeding season, these birds develop long plumes of feathers on their back, and their bill turns from bright yellow to black.

2. Common raccoon With their foxlike faces, black eye masks, and ringed tails, raccoons are instantly recognizable. They usually hunt at night, feeding on frogs, crabs, fish, birds, and eggs.

3. Striped skunk Most skunks warn away their enemies by stamping their feet, raising their tails, and walking stiff-legged. If this fails, they will spray the intruder with a foul-smelling liquid.

4. American mink Close relatives of weasels and polecats, minks live in waterside dens. They see poorly under water, but their partly webbed feet help them to swim well. They are often bred in captivity for their fine fur coats.

5. Grizzly bear Grizzlies love water and are keen salmon catchers, grabbing the fish with their teeth or claws. The female teaches the cubs to fish when they are a few months old. These huge beasts are now endangered in many areas due to hunting and loss of habitat.

6. Bald eagle These fish eagles are usually found inland by rivers and lakes. They have a spectacular courtship ritual in which they lock talons in midair and turn somersaults.

Their nests, added to year after year, can be 8 feet deep and 12 feet wide.

7. Coyote Also known as prairie or brush wolves, coyotes live alone or in small packs. They keep in touch with each other using a wide range of calls, from their well-known howls to yelps, barks, and wails.

8. River otter North American or Canadian river otters call to each other using short chuckles and chirps. They are keen hunters, feeding on frogs, crayfish, crabs, and fish.

9. Beaver Members of the rodent family, beavers have a stable social system. The male and female form a long-term partnership and both parents care for the young, called kits or pups, for up to 2 years.

10. Wolf Pack members hunt together and will run down deer and caribou. Each wolf has a place in the order of the pack, which is maintained by gestures and postures. For example, the leader of the pack – the dominant male – carries his tail higher than the others.

11. Osprey Sometimes called the fish hawk, the osprey is a keen hunter. When it sights a fish, it plunges feet forward into the water and grasps its prey in both feet. Small spikes on the soles of its feet help it grip its slippery meal.

12. Salmon As salmon migrate upstream to lay their eggs, the lower jaws of the breeding males become hook-shaped. The eggs are laid in a redd, or heap of stones, formed by the female lashing her tail.

13. Moose The largest deer, the moose has a broad drooping muzzle, a large flap of skin (the bell) hanging from its throat, and enormous branched antlers. The males have fierce mock fights, clashing and locking their antlers.

DESERT WASTES

As the sun goes down, many animals make their way to an oasis in the Sahara desert. Some animals have already arrived; others are on their way. Which ones make it to the cooling water?

1. Dromedary (one-humped camel) The camel does not store water in its hump but in its stomach lining. It can go for days without water and lose up to 27 percent of its body weight without being harmed. A camel can make up this loss in 10 minutes – one reportedly drank over 5 gallons of water in a few minutes.

2. Caracal The caracal, or desert lynx, usually hunts at night. Caracals feed on young kudus and small antelopes as well as jerboas, hares, and various birds. They can leap 6 feet up and strike down a bird in midair.

3. Scimitar oryx These beautiful antelopes are hunted for their long, gracefully curving horns. Although they can go without water for several days, scimitar oryx usually move south to slightly cooler areas in the dry season. They live in small groups and feed mainly on grass. They may look gentle, but the males are fierce fighters. The males and females have mock battles during courtship. They lower their heads and lock horns, pushing each other in circles. The pair may spin around over 20 times.

4. Desert jerboas Desert jerboas live in deep underground burrows. They use their front teeth and short front legs to dig and their long hind feet to kick away the sand. Jerboas leap across the desert on their hind feet and use their tail for balance. They do not drink water because they get all they need from the food they eat.

5. North African gerbil Living in groups of about 12, these gerbils hide by day in simple burrows dug in the sand. They emerge at dusk to search for seeds and plants, jumping across the desert on their long back legs. Like jerboas, they get water from the food they eat, so they do not need to drink.

6. Fennec The smallest fox, measuring about 14–15 inches from nose to tail, it has ears about 6 inches long, which help it to keep cool. It shelters in burrows in the sand, emerging at nightfall to feed on birds, insects, and lizards.

7. Spotted sandgrouse The size of small pigeons, these beautifully marked birds have short legs with feathers extending down to the toes. Sandgrouse are strong fliers and flock to a water hole at the same time every day. Some sandgrouse lay their eggs in the footprints of large animals, such as camels; others nest in small depressions. The male and female incubate the eggs and bring the chicks food and water.

8. Spiny agamas These lizards live in the dry desert areas of North Africa. Deserts are cold at night, and the lizards get so cold that they cannot move around much. However, as the sun heats the desert sand, the agamas warm up too and start moving and hunting again. They shelter under shrubs during the hottest part of the day. Spiny agamas usually chase and catch small insects, but they also eat grass, seeds, and berries.

9. Addax These shy antelopes have long spiral horns that can reach almost 3 feet in length. The horns are so highly prized by hunters that addax are now rare in the wild, but they are being bred in many zoos. Addax can survive in the depths of the desert, where the only sources of water are the grass and seeds that they eat, but they will drink large amounts of water when it is available.

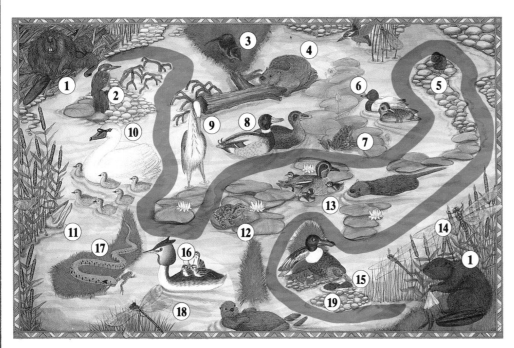

ON THE RIVER

*The peace of the river is broken by the female beaver's alarm signal.
Her mate has to get through the river maze and return to the dam.
But he doesn't want to disturb the other animals and must
find a clear pathway to his lodge.*

1. European beavers Once hunted for their beautiful fur, European beavers are now quite rare. Like North American beavers, they build vast dams of felled trees, mud, and stones which turn streams into pools.

2. Kingfisher The brilliant jewel-like colors of this bird shimmer as it dives below the water to seize fish in its sharp beak.

3. Water shrews These tiny creatures live in the riverbank. They mark their tunnels with scent from special glands on their backs to warn other animals away.

4. Otters The webbed feet of these sleek animals help them to swim at up to 7 miles per hour. They can stay underwater for up to 4 minutes.

5. Water voles Often called water rats, these shaggy creatures paddle along using all four feet to swim.

6. Pochards A diving duck, the pochard builds its nest in a mound of reeds in which the hen lays up to 17 eggs.

7. Natterjack The male's loud mating call can be heard over a mile away. These toads mate at night; the female lays strings of up to 4,000 eggs in the water. The eggs hatch into water-living tadpoles that metamorphose, or change, into adults, which live most of their lives on land.

8. Mallard During courtship, the bright male and the duller female preen each other's bright blue wing patches.

9. Gray heron Herons often wade into the water to search for fish, but they will also eat young birds, eggs, snakes, and plants.

10. Mute swan One of the heaviest flying birds at up to 50 pounds, these birds mate for life, both parents caring for the young.

11. Pike The pike's mottled skin makes it difficult to see as it hides among the reeds. A ferocious hunter, it darts out to trap its unsuspecting prey of fish and birds.

12. Common frogs The adults live on land, returning to the water to mate. Unlike toads, their eggs are laid in clumps – but develop into adults in a similar way.

13. Teal These small ducks are usually found in flocks. They often fly in formation, turning and landing together.

14. Emperor dragonfly Active hunters, these insects have a 4-inch wingspan and a body almost 3 inches long.

15. Shoveler As this duck swims, it sucks water in through its flat, broad bill. As the water runs out, tiny plant and animal food is left behind.

16. Great crested grebes Before they mate, both birds perform a complicated dance. They wag their heads, display their wings, and give each other water weeds.

17. Grass snake An active hunter, it preys on frogs, toads, and newts. Although it produces a poison that can kill small animals, it usually swallows its prey alive.

18. Banded demoiselle The pearly patches on this damselfly's wings make them look banded as it flutters among the flowers.

19. Brown rat Originally from Asia, brown rats are found wherever people live. They are serious pests and can carry disease.

THE OUTBACK

The call of a dingo has frightened three baby kangaroos as they play in the Australian bush. They make their way back to the safety of their mothers' pouches. But which joey belongs to which kangaroo?

1. Koala The tree-dwelling koala lives in dry forests on the edge of the bush. It eats only the leaves and shoots of a few species of eucalyptus, and an adult will consume over 2 pounds of leaves a day.

2. Princess parrot Although a rare bird, this parrot can be found throughout the interior of Australia wherever there is scrubland. Rarely seen, this beautiful bird is now protected by law.

3. Wedge-tailed eagle Australia's mightiest bird, it soars high in the sky waiting to dive, talons outstretched, on unsuspecting rabbits and other small mammals.

4. Kookaburra The largest of the kingfishers, it eats anything from insects to small mammals and birds. Its noisy, laughing call breaks the silence at dawn and at dusk.

5. Sulfur-crested cockatoo Flocks of these noisy birds may number up to 100 in the open plains. They fly to daytime feeding grounds and return to their roosting sites at night.

6. Dingo Descended from domestic dogs introduced by the Aborigines thousands of years ago, dingos usually feed on sheep and rabbits, although a pack will attack kangaroos, especially joeys.

7. Mallee fowl In winter, the male bird digs a pit in the ground and fills it with dead plants. He covers this with sand, and as the plants rot they give off heat. The bird tests the temperature, keeping it about 90°F by opening up the mound to cool it, or adding more sand to keep it warm. The female lays her eggs in holes in the mound, and the male looks after them until they hatch.

8. Gould's goanna Sometimes called the sand monitor, the large, 5-foot long goanna feeds on insects, birds, small mammals, and reptiles.

9. Emus Emus are large, flightless birds. The male incubates the eggs, rarely leaving the nest for the 8 weeks it takes them to hatch. He cares for the chicks until they can look after themselves.

10. Moloch Also known as the thorny devil, this harmless lizard is covered with a mass of spikes on its body, tail, and legs to protect it from its enemies. It feeds on ants, crushing their hard bodies with its flat teeth.

11. Red kangaroo These majestic animals travel into the bush after the rains, when food is plentiful. They move on their back legs, bounding across the land at speeds of over 12 miles per hour. The joeys, weighing less than 3/100 ounce at birth, stay in the pouch for several months, often returning there when danger threatens.

12. Hairy-nosed wombat This scrubland animal builds burrows that stretch for more than 40 feet underground. The female gives birth in the autumn, and the young wombat remains in the pouch for up to 3 months.

13. Frilled lizard When threatened, this spectacular reptile opens its mouth wide and unfolds the large frill around its neck. It runs across the ground on two legs, hunting for insects and other small animals.

14. Greater bilby The soft, blue-gray bilbies, or rabbit-eared bandicoots, live in deep burrows underground. They emerge at night to feed on seeds, bulbs, and insects.

IN THE JUNGLE

Deep within the rain forest of South America, a group of squirrel monkeys are climbing through the treetops. Below them they spy the juicy, golden fruits of the guava tree. But how can they reach the fruit without disturbing the other creatures of the forest?

1. Toucans The toucan's bill is huge but light because its bony tissue is filled with air bubbles. Toucans pick up fruit with their long bills. Then, with a flick of the head, they toss the fruit into their mouths.

2. Squirrel monkeys These agile monkeys use their long prehensile (grasping) tails to grip the branches as they travel through the rain forest. Newborn babies hitch a ride on their mother's back.

3. Macaws These brilliantly colored birds, members of the parrot family, live in noisy, screeching flocks. They feed on fruits, nuts, and seeds – their strong beaks can even crack the hard shells of Brazil nuts!

4, 12. Tamarins These silky-soft monkeys have distinct tufts or manes of fur. Instead of grasping branches or swinging through the trees like most monkeys, they use their clawed fingers and toes for balance and run along the branches like squirrels.

5. Opossum Opossums are marsupials – their young develop in a pouch. The woolly opossum has large eyes and good eyesight. It feeds on fruit and nectar and is an agile climber, using its prehensile tail, as well as its hands and feet, to grasp branches.

6. Kinkajou The kinkajou has thick, short fur and a long prehensile tail. Although kinkajous usually feed on fruit, they also use their long, mobile tongues to lick up nectar and honey.

7. Sloths Sloths are renowned for their extraordinarily slow movements. They feed on leaves and spend much of their lives motionless, hanging upside down. Their green color, which comes from tiny plants that live on their fur, provides effective camouflage in the leafy treetops.

8. Boa constrictor Although it usually lives on the ground, the boa constrictor can climb trees by grasping the branches with its tail. It kills birds and small mammals by crushing or suffocating them within the coils of its body.

9. Ocelot The ocelot, prized for its beautiful coat, is one of the many small cats threatened with extinction. It usually hunts at night for small mammals, birds, and reptiles. During the day it sleeps, safely hidden among the foliage.

10. Tree boa The brilliant green boa is well camouflaged among the leaves as it waits coiled around a branch. From here, it can easily seize and kill birds, bats, and other unsuspecting prey with its sharp teeth.

11. Jaguar The largest cat of the New World, the jaguar is a powerful hunter. It usually hunts on the ground, but it is an excellent climber and will pursue its prey of monkeys and birds through the trees.

13. Anaconda Anacondas usually live in swampy fresh water, but they can climb small trees. They often lie in wait for their prey, striking quickly to envelop it in their coils and drag it into the water.

14. Parakeets These noisy forest dwellers climb among the trees using their hooked beaks as well as their feet. Before they start to feed, parakeets often taste the fruit or seeds with their fleshy tongue.

AT THE WATER HOLE

It is just after sunrise and many animals are making their way to the water hole. A young zebra has become separated from the rest of the herd. It tries to get back to its mother, but there is only one safe route to take.

1. African elephants Their flexible trunks, actually an elongated nose and upper lip, are used for gathering food, drinking, smelling, and fighting.

2. Burchell's zebra Zebras live in herds and are active by day. They recognize each other by their stripe patterns as well as by sound and scent. Burchell's is the most common zebra in Africa.

3. Leopard Its beautiful spotted coat hides the leopard as it prowls through the trees and sleeps among leafy branches.

4. Impala This fleet-footed antelope can leap as high as 10 feet and as far as 33 feet. The males have long lyre-shaped horns; the females are hornless.

5. Cheetah The fastest land animal, this graceful cat can reach speeds up to 60 miles per hour over short distances.

6. Thomson's gazelle Small and graceful, these gazelles are easily recognized by the dark stripes along their sides.

7. Black wildebeest Herds of black wildebeest migrate up to 600 miles in search of food and water.

8. Ostrich Too big to fly, the ostrich is the fastest creature on two legs, running at up to 40 miles per hour.

9. Greater kudu Female kudus are usually hornless; the males have long spiraled horns.

10. Hoopoe A ground-dwelling bird, the hoopoe usually holds its huge crest flat, raising it only when alarmed or courting.

11. Hippos Hippos wallow in mud to keep cool. They can even walk underwater.

12. Secretary bird This long-legged bird may walk up to 50 miles a day in search of its prey of insects, snakes, and small rodents.

13. African wild dog Packs of hunting dogs roam over a wide area looking for prey. They work together to kill large animals such as antelope and wildebeest.

14. Topi The most numerous of African antelopes, topis can go without water for up to 30 days.

15. Giraffe The giraffe's long neck allows it to reach the highest leaves, but when it drinks, it has to spread its front legs wide and lower its head to reach the water.

16. Hamadryas baboon The male, twice the size of the female, has a heavy mane on his head and shoulders.

17. Black rhinoceros Rhinos often wallow in mud to keep cool. The mobile upper lip is used for grasping leaves and twigs.

18. Warthog Although the upper tusks are larger, the warthog uses its small, sharp lower tusks in fighting.

19. Lion The females of a pride (group) of lions do most of the hunting, killing their prey with a bite to the neck.

20. Nile crocodile After seizing its prey, the crocodile holds it underwater to drown it.

21. White stork These storks nest in Europe, then migrate south to spend the winter in Africa.

ON THE REEF

The waters of Australia's Great Barrier Reef are home to thousands of amazing and beautiful sea creatures. Here a jewel-like banded angelfish is trying to return to its shelter near the other angelfish, but in the way are hungry enemies and other creatures of the reef.

1, 22. Angelfish; 4, 10, 12. Butterflyfish Each kind of angelfish and butterflyfish has a special pattern of bright colors. Scientist Konrad Lorenz discovered that these colors acted as a warning, telling other fish to keep out of their territory.

2. Octopus Hiding among the rocks and corals, the octopus uses its eight long arms with their powerful suckers to defend itself against enemies and pull its prey into its fearful beaked jaws.

3. Portuguese man-of-war As the wind catches its large air-filled float, this colorful jellyfish is swept across the water's surface. Beneath the waves trails a mass of beautiful but poisonous tentacles, which trap unsuspecting prey.

5. Barracuda Fast-moving adult barracudas, with their needle-sharp teeth, are fearsome predators. They swim in schools (groups), attacking fish and other sea creatures.

6, 15. Starfish These colorful starfish move across the reef using hundreds of tiny sucker-like tube feet on the underside of their five arms.

7, 8. Clownfish; sea anemone Hidden safely among the anemone's stinging tentacles lives the clownfish. The anemone protects the clownfish from its enemies, and in return the clownfish chases away other fish that feed on the anemone's soft tentacles.

9. Beaked coralfish The bright stripes of the coralfish confuse its enemies by breaking up its outline and disguising its eye. A large, bright eyespot near its tail adds to the confusion, making would-be predators think that the tail's the head.

11. Lionfish The lionfish's amazing array of fins and stripes helps to camouflage it. At night it emerges to hunt, killing small fish with the poison in its spines.

13. Eagle ray As it moves across the reef, the eagle ray feeds on shellfish, crushing them with its powerful teeth. It defends itself by lashing its enemies with its tail, which is armed with a poison spine.

14, 17, 21. Corals Despite their rocklike appearance, coral reefs are formed from the limestone skeletons of millions of tiny animals. The living corals are small animals called polyps. They have a mouth at the top surrounded by stinging tentacles, which they spread out to catch food.

16. Sea horse The armored sea horse is most unusual: in the breeding season the female lays her eggs in the brood pouch of the male fish. After 4 to 5 weeks the male "gives birth" to perfect tiny sea horses.

18. Stonefish The stonefish lies half-buried waiting to ambush its unsuspecting prey. Its needle-sharp poison spines protect it from its enemies and kill the fish on which it feeds.

19. Grouper The strong jaws of these large fish are armed with sharp, backward-pointing teeth. Groupers snap up any animal that ventures into their territory, and they can change their color to match the corals in which they hide.

20. Blue shark These fast-swimming streamlined predators search for prey among the corals. They will attack most animals, from small fish to other sharks and octopus.

LIFE UNDERGROUND

In this European woodland clearing at twilight, many nocturnal (active at night) animals have emerged to search for food. The mother rabbit has to find the route through the maze back to her nest. But the weasel, fox, and other predators — as well as their intended prey — are barring her way.

1. Kestrel A common bird of prey in Europe, the kestrel is a master of hovering flight. It hangs almost motionless in the air, searching the ground below for the slightest movement. Then it swoops, catching its unsuspecting prey in its sharp talons.

2. Gray squirrel A relative of rats, these agile climbers spend much of their lives in the trees. They build their dome-shaped nests, called dreys, out of twigs, and line the dreys with moss and grass.

3. Badger A member of the weasel family, the badger is easily recognized by its distinctive black and white striped face. Groups of up to twelve live together in a large underground network of tunnels called a sett. The badger has very poor eyesight but an excellent sense of smell. It usually feeds on plants, earthworms, and other small creatures, but it will dig out and eat young rabbits if it finds them.

4. Rabbit This furry mammal lives in family groups in a vast network of underground tunnels or burrows called a warren. The female rabbits, called does, rear their young in the central part of the warren in nests lined with fur and dried grass.

5. Mole The enormous front feet of the velvety-coated mole are ideally suited for digging through soil. Moles spend most of their life underground. Excellent hunters of earthworms and other similar creatures, they eat about half their own body weight in food each day.

6. Fox Well known for their beautiful long, bushy tails, or brushes, foxes are most active at dusk and at night. Solitary hunters, they will eat almost anything, but they prefer young rabbits and rodents. Their young, called cubs, are born in early spring in well-hidden dens.

7. Tawny owl One of the most common owls in Europe, its ghostly call of "to-whit, to-whoo-oo" breaks the silence of the night in early spring. Sharp eyesight and a keen sense of hearing help it hunt its prey even on the darkest night.

8. Hedgehog The hedgehog, found in Europe, hibernates (sleeps) in winter, emerging in the spring to feed on worms, slugs, beetles, and snails. When in danger, a hedgehog rolls itself up into a tight ball.

9. Dormouse So called because in the winter it is dormant, or hibernates, the dormouse lives in European woods. It wraps its tail around its head and, except for an occasional meal from its store of nuts, stays in its nest until spring.

10. Stoat In winter the stoat grows a white coat and is called an ermine. In the spring it molts (sheds its fur) and grows red-brown fur on its back with a cream-white belly and black tips on its long tail. It feeds on small mammals such as rabbits, which are often paralyzed by fear at the sight of it and make no attempt to escape.

11. Weasel Unlike the stoat, the weasel keeps its red-brown coat all year and has a short tail. Small enough to chase its prey deep into the burrow, it eats rats and mice, but it will also kill young rabbits.

12. Adder The broad black zigzag line along its back and the black spots on its sides identify the poisonous adder, or European viper. Just one bite paralyzes the small animals on which the adder feeds.

PATHWAYS IN THE SNOW

As the summer sun warms the frozen Arctic tundra, the snow melts and for a brief time flowers bloom and animal life abounds. As daylight fades, the female lemmings and their pups must return to their burrow. But only one path leads to home.

1. Caribou These North American reindeer travel over 600 miles twice a year between their summer and winter feeding grounds. Their habit of digging through the snow to find food led the Micmac Indians to call them *caribou*, meaning "shoveler."

2. Arctic wolf Fierce hunters, a pack (group) of Arctic wolves may travel over 600 miles as they hunt caribou. Their ghostly howls keep them in touch with one another and warn other packs to stay away.

3. Pomarine jaegers These summer visitors breed on the tundra, feeding on lemmings. They lay up to three brown eggs, which hatch into mottled honey-brown chicks.

4. Ringed seal In the winter, when ice covers the seas, ringed seals use the long sharp claws on their front flippers to cut holes in the ice. After diving to hunt fish, the seals surface at these holes to breathe.

5. Snowy owl Daytime hunters, snowy owls feed on Arctic hares and lemmings. They nest in May in small hollows lined with moss and feathers. The male feeds the female while she incubates the eggs.

6. Musk ox Their long, shaggy coats and dense underfur keep them warm in the freezing Arctic winter. When threatened, they form a tight circle, with their heads and horns pointing at the enemy.

7. Arctic fox In its smoky gray summer coat, the Arctic fox blends in with its background. Its short ears and muzzle and furry-soled feet help to keep it warm in the freezing snow, and its snow-white winter coat conceals it from its enemies and its prey.

8. Canada goose When these large birds migrate to their breeding and summer feeding grounds, they always follow the same route and often breed in the same area where they were born.

9. Arctic hare Easy to recognize with their black-tipped ears and long hind legs, these hares usually live alone. They rest in small burrows in the ground or in shallow depressions called forms. In the winter they grow a white coat.

10. Polar bears Excellent swimmers with "webbed" toes, polar bears spend most of their lives hunting seals among the ice floes. In summer, they journey across the land, feeding on lemmings and plants.

11. Trumpeter swan These beautiful birds breed on the tundra, laying their eggs on a nest of grass and moss lined with swan's down. When the young are less than 90 days old, they make the long journey south to spend the winter in a warmer climate.

12. Walrus The walrus uses its snout and tusks (long front teeth) to pry shellfish from the ocean floor. The food is then gathered into the mouth by the mobile lips.

13. Lemmings These little animals are active even in the winter, feeding on seeds and plants they find in their snow tunnels. They usually have two litters a year. At times the number of animals increases so enormously that they have to find new places to live. They often swim across lakes and rivers and may even try to swim the sea.

TO THE SEA

As the newly hatched green turtles make their way to the sea, they are confronted by many dangers — raccoons, coatis, and gulls, which will eat them, and the twinkling lights of a nearby town which confuse them. Only a few of the hatchlings will reach the safety of the sea.

1. Green turtle At nesting time, green turtles travel hundreds of miles to lay their eggs on the beaches where they were born. The female makes a hollow in the sand with her front flippers. Lying in this hollow, so that her shell is level with the sand, she digs a deep hole with her hind flippers and lays over 100 eggs. She covers the nest with sand and returns to the sea. The eggs hatch 2 to 3 months later. The hatchlings dig their way out and head for the sea. Many die. The green turtle is now an endangered species because it has been hunted for its eggs, hide, and meat, and is losing its habitat along the beach.

2. Coati Although they usually live in woods and lowland forests, coatis will venture onto beaches to hunt for food.

The coati snuffles in the ground with its long, mobile snout, feeding on insects, spiders, and small animals. It will also dig up and eat turtle eggs as well as the young hatchlings.

3. Robber crab The robber crab weighs up to 5 pounds and is half a yard long. It climbs trees, feeding on fruit and coconuts.

4. Land crab These square-bodied crabs feed on both plants and animals. They live mainly on land, only occasionally returning to the sea.

5. Ghost crab This sand crab lies in burrows beneath the sand with just its long eyestalks visible. It usually feeds on sand flies but also attacks newly hatched

turtles, catching them by a flipper and dragging them underground.

6. Raccoon The raccoon hunts at night, using its front paws and long fingers to handle its food. It climbs well and can also swim. It usually lives in woods and swamps near water but also forages on beaches, digging up turtle eggs and hunting for hatchlings.

7. Spectacled parrotlets Found throughout Central America, these small parrots live in noisy, chattering flocks of between 5 and 20 birds. They live in open forest, feeding on berries, buds, blossoms, and fruit.

8. Yellow-headed parrots Good talkers, these bright, colorful parrots are under threat because they are collected in large numbers for the cage-bird trade. They are also in danger from the destruction of their forest homes.

9. Black skimmers Skimmers have a special way of catching fish. They fly just above the surface of the sea so that their flattened lower bill cuts through the water. When a skimmer comes upon a fish or crab, it snaps its upper bill closed, pulls it head sharply back to swallow its prey, and keeps on flying. In spring, when skimmers breed, the female scrapes out a hollow in the sand in which she lays 2 to 4 eggs.

10. Black-headed gulls These small, active gulls feed on almost anything. Their black heads are part of their breeding plumage. Colonies of gulls nest on marshes and coasts in the spring.

11. Magnificent frigate bird This beautiful bird catches its prey of fish, crabs, and, on this occasion, baby turtles by swooping down on them. The male has a large red throat pouch which he blows up like a football to attract females.